AN ARCANE AMIGO

CAME TO CHANGE THE FUTURE

RAMYA GUMADAVELLY

Made with ♥ on the Notion Press Platform
www.notionpress.com

This book is dedicated to all the dreamers who fight each day to turn the fictional stories in their heads into realities in their lives.

Contents

About The Author

Ramya Gumadavelly is a writer and software developer with a passion for astronomy, space exploration, and technology. A graduate in Computer Science and Engineering from SRMAP in 2021, she has always been captivated by the mysteries of the universe, which inspired her to write articles about time travel and black holes for space magazines. This fascination eventually led her to create her debut book, An Arcane Amigo.

Ramya has also co-authored anthologies like Letter from Home and Wild Woman. Outside of her professional and writing pursuits, she enjoys watching cricket, sitcoms, and taking long walks while having deep conversations with people. A huge fan of Virat Kohli and Steve Jobs, she admires their perseverance and innovative spirit, which motivate her in her own life and work.

Ramya finds great inspiration in Taylor Swift's writing. Her ability to blend emotions with storytelling is something that deeply resonates with Ramya, who believes that words have the power to heal and connect people across experiences.

With a heart full of dreams, Ramya is passionate about encouraging others to follow their heart and carve their own path in life. She believes that no dream is too big and that writing is one of the most powerful ways to share and inspire.

Preface

I don't even remember how small I was when I first became fascinated by space, aliens, and UFOs. Time travel, aliens, teleportation, black holes—everything about them has always captivated me. I was just 9 years old when I started searching for aliens on Mars online, memorizing the names of planets and their moons, and learning about their revolution times. I was obsessed with it all. Even now, nothing brings me more peace than watching a sky filled with stars. It's the most beautiful thing in the world.

I'm also a technophile, so the combination of space and technology is what keeps me up at night. I'm a writer too, and this book is the result of all the things I love.

I started with a short story, and thanks to the encouragement of my friends, I found the courage to expand it into a book and actually publish it. I promise you, it's not as scary as I imagined it would be in my head. So, if you have any crazy ideas, go for it! I promise it will be worth it—just like reading this book.

Love,
Ramya Gumadavelly

Foreword

In a world increasingly driven by technology, we often find ourselves at a crossroads between progress and preservation. An Arcane Amigo takes us on a gripping journey that explores the boundaries of human ingenuity and the unintended consequences of pushing those boundaries too far. Through the eyes of the protagonist, we witness not only the exhilaration of discovery but also the painful realization of how easily technology can shape our lives—both for good and for ill.

As the story unfolds, it reveals a powerful message about the importance of balance: how we must use technology not as a crutch or a replacement for the beauty of life's simple moments, but as a tool to enhance the world around us. With themes of friendship, courage, and redemption, An Arcane Amigo reminds us that our choices have consequences, and it is in our hands to shape the future.

This book is not just a work of science fiction, but a reflection on our own present-day struggles and the future we are all creating. It challenges us to think deeply about the direction in which we are heading and to recognize the responsibility that comes with the power to change the world.

About The Book

If you ever happened to meet an alien, if you are given a chance to travel through time, if you are given a chance to disappear and appear at any place you want, what would you do? How will you use these powers?

This thought-provoking question is the core of this science fiction story, An Arcane Amigo. This book revolves around some interesting science fiction mysteries and crisis people would face after inventing some revolutionary technology.

This book takes you through the journey of an enthusiastic girl with her mysterious friend and hurdles they face in every page of their journey with some nail-biting suspense. It makes you dive into the future world and make you realize the power that technology will give you and how it affects each and everyone's life. Don't wait for the future when you can feel it right now.

CHAPTER ONE

A Friend From A Far Land

I always thought life was boring, but for the past year, many things have happened in my life, and there have been many changes. I cried, laughed, and sometimes felt terrified, but it was a fantastic journey, and I just want to put it down in a book. That way, this journey, filled with fun and thrill, will last with me forever.

It was just another night in 2015, the sky filled with a million stars, clearly visible from my window. Watching the stars gives me butterflies, and I feel a rare peace in my heart. As part of my daily routine, I sat in my chair to write about my annoying day in the diary. I had a really bad day—nothing so special or exciting that was worth mentioning. Stargazing was the only thing I enjoyed; I just love getting lost in the stars. My days haven't really been different for the past few months. Every day, I've been living in the same space-time continuum: boring life, terrible exams, and worse marks. I really love physics. I'm passionate about the stars, the moon, and finding the origin of the universe. I really want to explore this vast universe and meet some aliens. I sound crazy, but that's who I am.

How great would it be to see a UFO, go to another planet? Maybe I could have my own planet where I don't have to write exams. See, again, I went into dreams. This happens to me in class too, maybe that's why my grades are low. Even though I love physics, I never scored good marks in that subject because all they ask is about a man running behind a bus and how fast he can catch it, which never inspired or fascinated me. But particles of light beams, photons traveling from the past, made me fall in love with this subject. This is me, an astrophile. I'm Alice, and I feel there's nothing more interesting to share about me. A few people worth mentioning in my life are my one and only friend, John, and my mom and dad. John and I spent our entire childhood searching for aliens on Mars on the internet instead of playing. We never found them, but we lost our eyesight. John is a geeky guy with an extreme love for coding and hacking. As time passed, our interests grew apart. My mom and dad both work for a big multinational company. They are like birds captured in a glass castle. They are always busy, and I hardly find them sitting peacefully and having a cup of coffee. They barely spend any time with me. They are a bit irritated with my actions and marks, but rarely do they have time to discuss them. So, in that way, I am safe.

I was really exhausted after this long day, so I just lay down on my bed. Suddenly, I heard a knock on the door. I went to open it, and to my utmost surprise and shock, it was my dad with my grade card. His face was red with anger, and I thought I was surely going to die that day. He didn't scold me but seemed very upset about my marks. He said, "We're not having time to take care of you, so you are making such mistakes. It's our fault, not yours," and he left the room. I felt very sad after that and decided to study hard, even though I didn't like the subject. I took out my books and sat at my study table. I started studying, but I couldn't concentrate. My thoughts were traveling all over the universe. Suddenly, I saw something glowing brightly in the sky and moving faster. I thought it was just my imagination, so I closed the window and tried to study again. But the glance had registered in my mind, and I couldn't believe it was just my imagination. I opened the window again and searched the sky for that object, but I couldn't see anything. Suddenly, I saw something weird in the sky, but I could not recognize it. So, I went and grabbed the telescope from my desk and set it up near the window. When I looked through the telescope, I couldn't believe my eyes. I saw a UFO moving fast. I thought it was a prank or a movie shoot, but deep in my heart, I felt like this should be real. But I was a bit terrified too. Millions of thoughts were crossing my mind, and I felt like going to bed. With my mind full of thoughts, I couldn't sleep. I consoled myself and went to sleep.

Suddenly, I heard an intense sound and woke up from my sleep. It was around 2:30 AM, and I had a very bad nightmare. Then, I saw a lot of light coming into the room from the window. I went out of the room; my parents were in a deep sleep. So, I gathered all my courage and opened the door. I was really shocked; I couldn't move an inch. I saw a gigantic UFO in my lawn. I just couldn't process it in my mind, being a physics lover, and believe that all these things really exist. I fainted.

After some time, I woke up. I was on my bed and just got relaxed, thinking this was all a sci-fi dream. I thought of going to the washroom and got down from the bed. I turned towards the washroom, and to my shock, there was an alien sitting beside me and staring at me. I decided I was done with all this nonsense, and with all the bravery I could muster, I tried to speak with the alien. It started to speak back to me, but I couldn't understand a single word. It was speaking in some alien language. But it could understand the fear and confusion on my face and tried to explain something to me in sign language. After a long struggle, the alien made me understand that it needed some help from me and that it wouldn't harm me at any cost. Then, I felt a little relaxed and accepted that everything happening wasn't a dream. I asked it, "How can I help you?" in sign language. The alien then asked me to stand still and look into its eyes. It suddenly sent some signals into my brain and captured the reflected signal in a small pill. I didn't feel anything painful or different. Then the alien swallowed the pill. It started speaking in my language. I was really shocked—how could a small pill have helped it learn the whole language in a second? I just felt, "Wow." Then, the alien said his name was Wart and that he was from a planet 45 million light years away from Earth. He said he came here to do a case study on this planet and its environment. His spaceship had some trouble, so it crashed in our lawn. He said he was also a student like me who loved to explore this world. He asked me to promise that I wouldn't tell anyone about meeting him, and that his visit to Earth should be kept confidential. He also said that if I fulfilled my promise, he would give me some amazing gifts that hadn't yet been invented on Earth. I promised him and assured him that I wouldn't tell anyone about this meeting. I also asked him to join me in his work so that I could learn more from him and help him finish his case study. At first, he was a little suspicious about me, but later agreed. We became friends. Then Wart explained to me how he learned my language. He said when he sent a signal to my brain, it actually stored all my language information in the reflected signal, which he then stored in a small edible chip in the form of a pill that he swallowed. I really loved that technology. Later, we started talking about our lives. Wart also loves exploring, but he isn't good at studies; he focuses more on projects than marks. That's why he risked his life and came all the way to Earth. But I didn't agree with him. I said, "You know many things and technologies that no one on Earth knows." He just laughed out loud and said these were basic things one should know on his planet. He didn't even know them properly. The conversation went on like that, and we started discussing many things about each other's planet and lifestyle.

Suddenly, I heard a loud scream outside the room. I stood up and ran to the living room. It was my mom—she saw the UFO in the lawn and started screaming. Wart and I were frightened, not knowing what to do. I went to my mom and pretended like nothing was in the lawn, but my mom wasn't listening to me. Wart went inside the UFO and tried to make it invisible, but since it had crash-landed, nothing was working properly. Meanwhile, I closed the lawn door and went into the kitchen to get some water. Then, I saw my mom calling the police. I went to her and tried to cut the call, but she had already informed them. I didn't know what to do. The police would be here in 10 minutes, and if Wart couldn't solve the issue in the UFO. If they saw him in the lawn, it would be a big problem for him. I asked my mom to sit in the bedroom. I went to Wart, and we tried many things, but nothing was working, not even his lockers. He said if he could get his devices out, he could do something. So, I ran into the storeroom and brought a hammer. Wart started hitting the locker, but it was very hard to open. I could hear the police approaching. I didn't know if we would escape from this trouble or not.

CHAPTER TWO

NOTHING IS EASY

We couldn't even breathe properly. My heart was beating faster than ever as the sound of the siren grew louder. A car stopped in front of my house, and all the police surrounded the UFO. With no choice left, Wart gave a strong hit on the locker, and it suddenly broke open. He said, "Alice, please go and manage the police, and I will take care of the rest." I went down to the police and started speaking, saying it was my car and I owned it, but no one believed me. How stupid of me? They drew their guns, and Wart just came outside the UFO. Everyone pointed their guns toward him. I thought we were done.

In the blink of an eye, there were no police around me, and the UFO was gone from the lawn. Wart was standing in front of me, giving me a big smile. I asked him out of excitement, "What happened?" He said he froze the time and took the police back to the station. He also shifted the UFO to a cave on the tallest mountain in the city, where people generally never go. He explained that most of his ancestors and friends who came to this city used to hide their vehicles in the same cave. I felt so relaxed.

Then I suddenly remembered my mom. I rushed into the house. The bedroom door was still locked. I opened it and saw my mom was still awake and seemed to be freaked out by everything that happened. I just pretended that all she saw was a dream and showed her that there was nothing in the lawn, and no police had come to the house, just to make her believe my lies. It actually worked well, and my mom went back to sleep. Then, Wart and I went back to my room.

We laughed, looking at each other's faces, and both of us said at the same time, "It all just started." But I really enjoyed these thrilling moments in my life more than boring classes. Wart said he would go to the cave and stay there, so no one could see him. He said we would meet tomorrow night and start our work, so no one could recognize him properly in the dark. I gave him my hoodie and pants so no one could guess he was an alien. He showed me his ring, which could teleport him to the cave in seconds. Within moments, he vanished from my sight.

I went back to my bed and slept, full of excitement for the next day. I woke up in the morning, full of enthusiasm. I was already late for school. So, I got ready quickly and boarded the bus. I saw many people discussing some alien stuff and speaking as if they had seen an alien last night. I was really terrified and thought it was surely about Wart. One of them even said the alien had been shot dead by someone. I was almost crying. I wanted to ask them for details, but I had no friends on the bus. The bus stopped in front of John's house, and he stepped into the bus and sat beside me. I controlled my tension and asked him why people were talking about aliens. He asked his friends, and they said there was a new science fiction movie that had been released yesterday, and they all went to see it. I just sighed long and felt like I was flying.

I went to school and waited the whole day for the night. In the evening, I came home, studied a bit, but I couldn't wait to meet Wart and tell him about the incident on the bus.

Around 12 o'clock, Wart came to my room. We sat down and discussed what had happened all day. He laughed about the bus incident. He said he was going to stay here for 15 days, and we figured out the places we would visit each night and planned to finish the whole case study as quickly as possible. He said he had informed his friends to send him another UFO, and it would arrive exactly on the 15th day. So, we tried to start things faster. I packed my laptop and a few other things in a backpack, covered myself completely, and went to the mountain first.

I asked Wart if he had eaten anything since morning. He showed me some pills and said those were his food. I laughed, but he said his planet was totally polluted, and no plants could be grown there. So, all the nutrients required for the body were taken as pills. I felt sad because that could be the future situation for us as well.

Days were passing, and each day we went to a new place, with Wart doing his work sincerely and me helping him now and then. Life was really exciting now; we were having long, meaningful conversations about the universe. I learned many things from him, and apart from physics, I grew interested in environmental studies too. When he explained the condition of his planet, I could imagine the condition of our planet in the future.

I think it was the 14th day of our plan, and Wart's case study was almost done. Our friendship had grown stronger over these days, and it was really hard for us to think that this was Wart's last day on Earth. We sat on the rooftop of my house, gazing at the stars and thinking about everything that had happened in the last 14 days. Suddenly, we noticed a light flash on us. We saw a man running with a camera in his hand. I asked Wart to go to the room, and I went down to catch him, but he ran very fast. I could only remember his face. I felt like I had seen this man somewhere before. I went back to the room, and as usual, we didn't know what to do. Wart said not to worry because even if he took a photo, it wouldn't be clear, and no one would believe it. But I felt we shouldn't take a chance. I tried remembering where I had seen him before. Suddenly, I remembered. Yes, his photo was in the newspaper this morning. I went to the room and brought the newspaper, and to our shock, he was a famous journalist who had recently won an award for his work. Now, Wart also started feeling tense. We tried searching for his details on the internet, but we couldn't find his address or phone number which is very strange. We couldn't think of anything else. Just one day left, and Wart would be gone from this planet, but we didn't know what could happen in these 24 hours. We just left things to destiny, and I asked Wart to go back to the cave. Neither of us could sleep the whole night.

The next morning, I woke up and didn't feel like going to school. I acted like I had a bad headache and told my mom I would stay home. She agreed, and my mom and dad left to the office. I went to say goodbye to them and found an envelope in the mailbox. I felt it was very strange. Inside, there was a pen drive. I rushed to my room, plugged it into my laptop, and was taken aback from the chair. There were many pictures of Wart, me, and the UFO. These were all taken on the first day when Wart came to my home. I was shocked. We didn't notice him that day; we were busy managing the police, my mom, and hiding the UFO. But both of us couldn't imagine this would happen. The evidence was very strong. If he released it, we'd be in big trouble. There was a message in the text document saying that he would release all the photos and videos unless I handed Wart over to him. I would never imagine doing that to him. He is my best friend. There were only a few hours left, and Wart would be in big trouble when the new UFO arrived. I ran as fast as I could to the cave.

I told Wart everything that had happened, and he was terrified, but he didn't want to see me in trouble. So, he said he would surrender to the journalist, but I didn't agree with him. I said we would figure things out and face the problem together. I went to the post office to find the journalist's address, and a man there helped me with it. I went to his house, but he wasn't there. When I asked the watchman, he said the owner had gone on vacation. I didn't know what to do. I searched many places, but I couldn't find him. It was already evening, and my tension grew stronger with each passing minute. I stopped near a shop to drink some water. There was news on the television that the famous journalist was going to show the true alien today. I freaked out when I saw this. Suddenly, I got an idea. Why don't we use the time freezer? Wart can freeze time and escape, then release it afterward. I ran to Wart and explained my idea. He said he had already thought of it, but the batteries were drained. I didn't know what to do. Time was moving faster, and Wart said he was working to fix some bugs in his program. Many thoughts were running through my mind. Can he solve it? Will we have a happy ending to our 15-day journey?

CHAPTER THREE

A Sad Departure

I was in a trance for some time, and my brain was filled with negative thoughts. I was really terrified. Suddenly, Wart shouted, "I fixed it." I came back to consciousness and asked what had happened. He said he had fixed the bugs in the program, which had the ability to erase certain parts of memory in our brains. On their planet, they generally use this to erase the worst memories from people's minds, helping them return to a normal psychological state. I felt a bit relieved, but we only had an hour left. Wart's UFO was approaching Earth. We had installed the program in a device that sends signals to our brain, altering neural pathways and erasing certain memories.

We ran as fast as we could, searching for the journalist. We couldn't find him, and we had no idea where he might be hiding. Suddenly, Wart said he could be near your house or the cave, because he already knew that the UFO could land at either of these places. I thought going to my house was the best idea because he had just posted the letter to my address. He may not know where Wart actually lives. So, we ran to my house. Our guess was absolutely correct—he was hiding in the house just behind mine, observing the sky through a telescope. But he was too far to send signals with high intensity. So, we went closer to him. He saw us and turned the camera towards us. We had no other choice but to take a risk. The journalist took out his phone and called a news channel. He stood directly opposite us and said, "I will become the greatest of all time, but you are going to be in big trouble."

Wart took his device and projected some high-intensity signals towards him. We didn't know if this would work, but we tried anyway. The journalist suddenly fainted. We heard some cars approaching, so we went to my house and opened the window to see whether our plan had worked. We left a small microphone near the journalist. Some people got out of the car and woke him up. When we heard them speaking, the people from the press asked him where the UFO and aliens were. The journalist said he didn't know anything about aliens or UFOs. They told him he had come to their studio that morning and said he would show them a real alien that night. The journalist said he didn't remember saying anything like that and also claimed he had never seen any UFOs. The people got irritated but couldn't do anything because he was a renowned journalist. They just left, and the journalist went back to his home. We gave each other a big high-five because our plan had worked perfectly. But we never thought to check things again. The consequences of our negligence were realized later.

It was 1 o'clock in the night, and we were waiting on the terrace for the UFO. I felt really sad and asked Wart not to leave me, to stay here forever. He laughed and asked me to come with him. Since both options were next to impossible, we decided to face this situation happily. As he had promised some gifts, he took a watch and a pill from his backpack and gave them to me. He had set some code in the pill and asked me to swallow it. It didn't taste good.

He asked me to say his name three times. I did so, and I could actually hear Wart's words and speak to him too. I was surprised and asked if it would work even when he was on the other planet. He said that was the reason he gave me the pill. This pill was used for telepathy, allowing people who had the same code in their pill to talk to each other. He also added that the watch was useful for time travel and teleportation. I felt really excited.

His UFO landed on my terrace, and our eyes filled with tears. It's always hard to depart from friends, but we had no other choice. He warned me to use the watch only when it was absolutely essential. We both hugged each other. I had never had such a good friend in my life, and I couldn't control my tears. I said goodbye to Wart and rushed into my room. Even Wart was very sad, so he went into his UFO and started his journey back to his planet. I watched through the telescope, and I saw the UFO vanish from my sight. It had been a beautiful journey of fifteen days, but the departure was horrible.

Fifteen days of excitement finally came to an end. I felt very relaxed and calm though. I went to sleep with great satisfaction. Life is full of surprises; one chapter ends, but another is about to start. Suddenly, I heard a knock at the door. I opened it, and it was my mom with my progress report in her hand. She was really upset. The same story was repeating itself, but this time, I started crying so I could avoid her scolding. Crying was the best way to escape anyone's anger. She pacified me for a while and left the room, saying the same dialogue for the thousandth time: "Try to get good marks next time."

Suddenly, my phone started vibrating. It was John. He called to remind me about tomorrow's test. He said the syllabus was huge, so he thought about hacking into our examination department's computer, but it was too difficult. So, he started studying to at least pass. I didn't even know the syllabus, so how would I escape this problem? I went to my desk and started studying. My mom was shouting from the living room, and her words woke me up. I hadn't even turned to the first page of my book when I realized I had fallen asleep. I decided to prepare for the worst day and started my way to school.

The exam was really tough. I couldn't solve a single question properly. I thought I should study well for the next exams. You know, when we take others' opinions or words seriously, we often end up doing things that are not right. That evening changed my life. I never thought I would make such unethical decisions. When my professors distributed the marksheets, I was the lowest scorer in the whole class. My professors asked me to stand up and humiliated me in front of the entire class. I couldn't hold my tears, so I ran to the washroom and cried for half an hour. Everyone in the class was laughing at me. I couldn't handle the humiliation. I went out to wash my face. None of my classmates cared about me, but John came over and consoled me. I felt a bit relieved.

I went back home but couldn't forget what had happened at school. I couldn't stop thinking about it. My mom and dad came home from work. The very first question they asked was, "How was the exam?" I didn't want to lie, so I told them the truth. They started scolding me, and I couldn't take it anymore. I ran to my room and locked the door. I cried my heart out. I hated myself. Then the only solution I found was to kill myself. I ran to the kitchen and took a knife. I gathered all my courage and put the knife to my wrist. Never make decisions when you're sad or angry because those emotions lead you to do things you should never do. It was the worst decision I ever made. It made me do things I should never have even dreamed of doing.

CHAPTER FOUR

A MAJOR CHANGE

I didn't kill myself. When I placed the knife on my wrist, I saw the watch that Wart gave me. Then I got a witty thought. I found a way to score good marks and implemented my idea immediately. I used the watch and traveled to the next day to see all the questions. I noted everything on a paper and came back to the present time. I read all the answers the whole night and prepared well for the exam. The next morning, I went to school with full confidence of scoring full marks, but to my utmost surprise, I forgot most of the answers. I didn't remember the complete answer for any question because I had memorized each answer but didn't understand any of them. So, I couldn't remember any of them properly. I decided to study the concepts related to the questions from now on. I went back home.

In the evening, I started going to all the places I love using teleportation. I enjoyed it a lot. I came back home at night. I completely forgot about the test the next day, but I didn't worry. I got another bad idea today. I took my book along and traveled to the time when the test ended and exactly when my professor placed the paper in the locker in her cabin. My timing was good—she didn't lock the locker, only the door. I teleported myself into the cabin, took my paper, filled in all the answers, and came back to the present time. The next day, I went to school and didn't write anything in the exam, but my plan worked well. I got full marks on the exam, everyone appreciated me, and my teacher was happy. I really loved that feeling of being appreciated. I was getting these by cheating, but I didn't care.

I went home and waited for mom and dad. I rushed to them as soon as they came home. I showed them my mark sheet. They also appreciated me, and mom made my favorite dishes for dinner. I really enjoyed that day. I lived in false happiness. I know, but I was slowly getting addicted to cheating. That night, John called me and said that the teacher was suspicious about my marks; he heard her speaking with other teachers. I said I didn't do any cheating, so there was no need to worry about anything. But after hanging up, I felt a bit tense, though I convinced myself that the teacher would never find out. The next morning, I went to school. My teacher called me to her cabin and asked if I had really worked hard to pass the test. I said I didn't make any mistakes with full confidence. She said, "Let's go to the CCTV room and check what happened in my cabin yesterday." I was terrified. If she watched the footage, she would know everything I did. I didn't know what to do. I would get suspended if she found out about my cheating. My heart started beating faster and faster as we moved toward the security room. I didn't even have a single idea.

Finally, we reached the room, and my teacher asked the security officer to show her the footage from the day after the exam. He opened his computer and started typing. The footage started playing, and only a few minutes were left—the truth would be revealed, and I would be expelled from school. Suddenly, I got an idea. I tried freezing time using the watch. Time stopped, everything around me froze, and only I could move. I tried deleting the video clips and succeeded. I unfroze the time. My professor saw the footage but couldn't find me in it. She apologized to me and appreciated me for my hard work. I laughed silently and went back to class.

From that day, I started seeing all the question papers before the exams and then just copying them. I got good grades and never bothered to study. I finished all my exams in the same way. Those fake good marks boosted my ego. I didn't care about John, I was very rude to him. Eventually, all my friends hated me, but I didn't care about them. I thought, *this watch is enough for me for my whole life*, but I didn't realize it was just a machine. I didn't even bother talking to Wart because he wouldn't like what I was doing with his watch.

Even if I had some problems in my life, I used to skip time and get rid of the situation. I didn't even spend time with my friends, anticipating future fights. Eventually, I was left alone. I never went anywhere on foot or traveled in a vehicle; I just used teleportation. As a result, I became fat and lazy. I skipped time every time I felt like not living the moment. I did it many times. Sometimes, I skipped weeks and months. I only wanted happiness in my life and didn't want to face any sad or bad situations.

One day, I wanted to go to a nearby shop. I could actually go by walk, but I used the watch and teleported myself onto the road. Suddenly, a car came and hit me. It was a terrible accident, and I suffered major injuries. I broke my leg. I couldn't bear the pain. I wanted to skip that part again, but this time, the watch stopped working. I tried hard, but it wasn't working. The doctor told my parents that, due to my overweight, there were many issues with my body. I had to go through a painful treatment and many days of rest to recover completely. My parents were really sad. I didn't know what to do. I felt really depressed. I didn't know how to face this situation. All the money they had earned over the years was being spent on my treatment. This was all because of my mistakes. I wanted to correct them but didn't know how.

Then, I sat on the bed, thinking about what to do. Suddenly, I remembered the pill and said Wart's name thrice immediately. It had been a year since I last spoke to him. I thought he would never reply, but within no time, Wart heard my words and started speaking. I told him my situation. He said I had made a big mistake in my life. Then, he made me realize what I had missed. Pain, failure, and the worst times are situations that teach us the most important lessons in life. I had skipped those and craved temporary happiness. I hadn't learned anything in life, and I didn't have anyone to support me either. My life was way better without this watch. I didn't work hard, so even though I succeeded, it didn't give me happiness. Good health is essential to live, and I had even lost that. After this realization, I pleaded with Wart to take me to the past or repair the watch. Wart said he could repair the watch only if I came to Earth. He said he would start immediately. If he could repair the watch, I thought I would go back to the day when Wart gave it to me and give it back to him. I promised to talk with Wart during his lone voyage to Earth. We kept talking about everything that had happened over the past year. I felt relaxed.

Suddenly, I couldn't hear him anymore. There was complete silence. I tried to speak to him, but I got no response. How should I meet him? Is he safe, or has something happened to the spaceship? All these questions kept running through my mind. After a long time, I heard some words, but I couldn't hear them clearly. Then, there was complete silence again. I heard a few more words: "Earth," "cave," "paper," and "watch." Only those words were clear. Wart was surely trying to tell me something, but I couldn't figure it out. I was sure he was in great danger. I was thinking hard, but I couldn't connect the dots. After a few minutes, I heard a few more words: "lab," "forest," and, at last, "save me, save me." I was terrified and broken. He had come to save me, but now he was in danger. I couldn't do anything except connect those words and try to figure out where he was. I finally got the connection. He was trying to say that he had reached Earth and gone to the cave where he used to live. But what was this paper? Suddenly, I realized it might be about the journalist, but we had erased all his memory. How could he remember about Wart? I didn't want to take a chance. I still didn't understand the connection between the lab and the forest, but I had to start immediately. I couldn't move from the bed with my broken leg, so I called John and pleaded him to help, telling him the whole story. He promised to help. He came to the hospital, took me in a wheelchair, hacked all the cameras so no one would figure out my absence, then took his car and started towards the cave.

CHAPTER FIVE

A MYSTERIOUS FOREST

It may be the darkest night I have ever seen; not a single star is visible in the sky. It is as gloomy as my life. John drove fast towards the cave, and we entered. It was completely dark, and we couldn't see anything. I noticed a stone shining in the darkness; it was the locket from Wart's chain. Then I realized my connection was correct, but I didn't know what to do next. The land was wet from the heavy rain last night. I took the torch from my bag and looked around. John shouted that he could see some footprints leading down the hill.

There were three types of footprints: one was definitely Wart's, and the others might belong to journalists, but whose footprint was the last one? John said we had to hurry up and stop wasting time thinking. We went down the hill and entered a big forest. No one dared to enter this forest because it was said to be dangerous. We were terrified, but we had no other option. I could hear the terrifying sounds of many animals, but we didn't see a single one on the way. The forest was strange; it felt like there were people living there. As we moved deeper, the intensity of the sounds increased. John opened his device and started tracing signals to detect if anything unusual was happening in the woods.

John said his device was showing a strong internet signal in the middle of the forest, and I wondered why anyone would need such a strong internet connection in the middle of nowhere. Then, John noticed a suspicious signal on the device, and it was approaching us faster and faster. John shouted, "Run! Faster!" Suddenly, a giant monster appeared before us. We couldn't move, frozen in fear. It was a fight-or-flight situation, and we chose to fight to save our friend. We tried to throw a knife at it, but it just passed through its body. It was strange. I thought this was the end of our story.

Then John laughed and walked near the monster. He actually walked through it. He said it was just a simulation designed to scare people who entered the forest. My suspicions about the forest grew stronger and stronger. John was very worried and suspicious that there might be an alien base in the forest, and that Wart had created all of this to trap us. I couldn't believe that Wart would do such things to his friends, but after what I saw in the forest, John's words seemed convincing.

I couldn't give up on my friend, so I convinced John, and we moved on. After moving a certain distance, we saw a bright light coming from a dome-like structure. We kept moving forward, and to my utmost shock, there were a few aliens standing in front of the door. I made the connection now; it was the same lab Wart had mentioned. John shouted at me to stop, warning me not to move forward. He pleaded with me to believe that Wart wanted to trap us and lead us into their alien base. I didn't agree with him, but to be honest, everything I was seeing made me consider his words. He grabbed my chair and insisted we leave, but I couldn't accept that Wart had betrayed me. I thought he was my only true friend. I couldn't stop myself from crying.

Suddenly, I heard a loud cry. I was certain it was Wart. I begged John to take me back to the base. My heart told me he was in big trouble. John turned my chair around, and we rushed toward the base. We stopped at a certain distance and waited for the alien guards to move inside. We could hear the cry again and again. I was sure it was Wart. I decided we had to save him, no matter the cost.

We threw a stone to the other side. One of the guards was sleeping, and the other went to check on the noise. We quietly approached the guard, tied him up, and gagged him. We took his ID card and entered the lab. Once inside, we noticed something strange about the guard—his skin felt like cloth, just like a costume. We took out a knife and demanded the truth from him. Terrified, he told us the truth: this was a research laboratory owned by a scientist named Mikinson. It was an illegal lab because the scientific society had banned him from conducting research. He used his technology to do evil things, so he was suspended permanently. Mikinson was conducting secret research here in the forest and didn't want anyone to know. The guards dressed up as aliens to scare people away from the forest, and the journalist and Mikinson were college friends. Mikinson offered the journalist a huge sum of money in exchange for capturing an alien. We gagged the guard, took his costume, and locked him in a room.

We started searching for Wart. Suddenly, we heard an evil laugh. We followed the sound and found him—Wart was lying on a bed, and they were trying to dissect his body. They had taken the telepathy pill and placed it aside on the table. We heard footsteps approaching. John hid me behind a pillar and went to speak to the human disguised in an alien costume. The man had a plate with a small pill and a glass of water, possibly medicine for the scientist. John stopped him, took the plate, and sent the guard away. John came back to me. With the plate, we could get inside, but how would we save Wart?

I had an idea. I asked John to swap the pill with the telepathy pill on the table and send the journalist outside by claiming there was something suspicious. John was unsure about the idea, but I asked him to trust me because we didn't have time to second-guess. I hid behind the pillar while John executed the plan. As soon as the journalist left, I locked the door. John came back outside, and Mikinson took the telepathy pill. I called out Mikinson's name three times and started speaking loudly, disrupting his concentration. I shouted at him, disturbing him mentally until he couldn't take it anymore and shot himself. The evil had come to an end.

We finally saved Wart. He was really happy. It would have been a big problem if Mikinson had completed his tests on Wart. It would have been dangerous for both mankind on Earth and their planet. Wart told us we needed to erase the journalist's memory again. I asked why it didn't work the last time. He explained there was a bug in the program. The memory had been erased from his conscious mind, but not from his subconscious. The journalist must have come to the cave to recollect his memories, but when he saw me, his subconscious recalled some scenes from the incident. Wart said he had fixed the issue.

We used the device to send a strong signal to the guard and the journalist. They fell unconscious. We did the same with the other guard and untied him. We ran as fast as we could to escape before they regained consciousness.

Finally, we reached the car. It was about 3 AM. Wart told me he had brought a new watch for me and took the old one. He explained that the watch could move time backward, but only those who touched the watch would remember what happened. Everyone else's life would stay the same. The three of us touched the watch and went back to the moment when Wart gave me the watch. I gave it back to him and kept the pill. Wart also gave one to John. I thanked him for everything. John was with us this time. His UFO arrived as before, and we waved goodbye to him as he went back home. I sat at my table, finished writing the story, and closed the book on my mysterious experiences.

After all these experiences, I realized something and figured out what I should do in my future. I'm really excited to share this with Wart and John. My idea isn't just about my life; it's about a better lifestyle for future generations, and it will only be possible if the three of us work together. Cheers to new beginnings for a great future.

CHAPTER SIX

FOR THE FUTURE

I realized my mistakes. I had misused and overused technology. I now understand the importance of living in the present and appreciating every moment of life. While technology has made many important and useful changes, we, becoming too accustomed to it, have lost the ability to enjoy the little things and maintain a meaningful social life. It was only after that incident that I recognized the darker side of technology and decided to work hard to avoid the problems the future world would face. I shared my idea with John and Wart, and both of them were happy about my change in perspective. We decided to work together to shape the future.

We planned to use the lab in the forest for our research. I learned many new things and worked on fascinating technologies such as time travel, teleportation, and quantum physics. I studied hard and achieved good grades. We worked every second, not just for ourselves but for future generations.

It was 2100 when we decided to introduce our technology to the world. Aliens and humans had already started collaborating. We founded the Interplanetary Space and Technology Club and introduced many innovative technologies, but with strict guidelines to prevent misuse and overuse. People began to use these advanced technologies, like time travel and teleportation, but all their actions were monitored by the club.

With the help of this club, I made sure that no one would repeat the mistakes I had made. Technology should improve a person's lifestyle, not deprive it. It's all in our hands and our attitudes. We have the power to either build or destroy the world using technology. I had that power in my hands, and I destroyed my life with it. But I was given another chance to correct my mistakes. Not everyone gets that opportunity. We must use the power in our hands to create wonders that have the ability to change the lives of mankind in the best way possible.

Dear Reader,

Thank you so much for taking the time to read this book to the end. This is my first book, and I hope it's the first of many. The fact that you decided to give it a try truly means a lot to me.

Writing is therapy. Sometimes, when you lack the courage or strength to speak your mind, expressing yourself through stories, poems, or any other form of art can be a powerful outlet. Every true experience of yours can give birth to countless fictional stories that have the power to heal many hearts.

If, at any point while reading this book, you felt like writing something down—or even if the thought just occurred to you—please do so. Trust me, there is a writer in all of us. All you have to do is pour your heart onto paper with your words. I firmly believe in the power of storytelling because one story I read once changed the way I viewed a situation in my life and helped me recover from a difficult period. It made me realize how important it is for each of us to write and share. Your story could inspire someone else and help them heal, too. So please, think about it.

Thank you again for reading my book. I hope my words have touched you in some way.

Ever in your love,
Ramya Gumadavelly

Other Titles By Ramya

There are countless feelings, adventures, and lessons throughout our lives. These are the beating hearts of our lives, which improve and enhance the beauty of our tale. Each of us possesses a writer within who yearns to express these unfiltered, genuine emotions to the world. Some of us, including myself, tune in. I hope that everyone who reads this book, which is a compilation of all those pieces of writing that I wrote from the bottom of my heart, will be moved by it.